DONNA ARP WEITZMAN

DEAR
MELANIA

LOVE ADVICE FROM A
RELATIONSHIP EXPERT

Other books by Donna Arp Weitzman

Cinderella Has Cellulite and Other Musings of a Last Wife

Sex & the Siren: Tales of a Later Dater

The Wind Blew Innocent: A Memoir

To all those wanting love and commitment

xo

Priscilla Purity

TABLE OF CONTENTS

INTRODUCTION

Although I spent most of my younger years in the very serious world of corporate sales, I find it amusing that I have also become an accidental love and dating relationship expert somewhere along the way. I wrote my first book, *Cinderella Has Cellulite*, about my perspective on marriage the second (or third) time around and shared some humorous stories from my own experiences. I had no idea then that I would soon be contacted to host my own radio show about relationships and be interviewed by radio and television hosts all around the country.

The overwhelming success of *Cinderella Has Cellulite* led to my second book, *Sex and the Siren*, and all the dilemmas single women find themselves in as "later daters." A few years ago, I was asked to write a love advice column for the *Katy Trail*, a local newspaper in Dallas where I live. The column was a hit, I imagine because everyone needs advice in this area once in a while, even if you've been married 20 years!

One day I was reading over some old published columns when it struck me that this timeless advice could be really amusing if you read it from the perspective of our modern society's obsession with President Trump's relationship with his seemingly normal wife, Melania. What if a self-proclaimed relationship expert and life coach wrote to the First Lady a series of letters to advise her on loving The Donald? That day Priscilla Purity was born! She may be stuck in her ways from a bygone era, but darn it if she doesn't have something to say to today's society about everything from love and sex to fashion advice for the First Lady.

I hope you'll have as much fun reading these as I did in re-writing them. You'll have to hold your tongue firmly in cheek as you read—and who knows? You may just pick up an idea or two about how to improve your own love and dating relationships.

Donna

Dear First Lady of the United States,

I am writing to you today to express my appreciation for the job you are doing as the First Lady. Goodness knows it's not an easy job. And I don't just mean being the one who decides what kind of consommé to serve at the next State Dinner. I think you know what I mean. I'm concerned as a citizen and as a fellow woman regarding the most important relationship a woman can have: her partner.

I've been giving love advice for quite a while now, and I had the idea the other day to write to you personally about some truths I've learned along the way. I hope you don't think I'm being too bold to share them with you. After all, sisters have to stick together, right?

If they help you even the teensiest bit, I can sleep at night knowing that I've done my civic duty. I've enclosed the first letter here. See what you think.

Sincerely,

Ms. Priscilla Purity
Love and Relationships Expert

Loving Your Political Opposite

♥

Dear Mrs. Trump,

The political climate is hot right now—to say the least. The President is making it hard to get along with friends who have differing political views, let alone romantic partners. But, love is love. If it's possible to find ways to agree to disagree and also treat President Trump with respect, your relationship might just work. However, there are things known as "deal breakers," and these are very real. They can drive a wedge between you, so I'm here to give you some tips to try before you two call it quits. After all, three times should be the charm for our new President!

First things first: be respectful. The fact that President Trump might have thought enough about the issues to find his stance on them should be attractive to you. It seems each of you is your own person, which means you both are allowed to have your own opinions. But, you might show more respect. Give President Trump space to be politically independent, without immediate repercussions.

Remind yourself that your partner is not the exact replica of the person you voted for. It's possible that he voted in the past for specific reasons—certain ones that may outweigh others. You likely agree with some things and disagree with others. It doesn't mean President Trump ran for office for himself. He likely thought you'd be a great asset.

The next step is to ask and listen. What better way to show you respect the President than by giving him the platform to speak and explain? Listen deeply, carefully, and patiently to his views and opinions. More importantly, do not listen with the goal of responding; listen to listen, even if it seems unlikely that you'll get a chance to do anything else. After all, yours is a mutual and equal relationship. Am I right?

Mrs. Trump, please keep things in perspective from the start. When you disagree, try to look at things from above. Remember who you're talking to: the President of the

United States. Someone you love and adore, even though you have some disparate ideas. Keeping things in perspective will keep you happier. Don't take certain things so seriously. It'll also keep your conversations productive.

Never be a bully. The worst thing you can do, no matter how you disagree, is be mean or hateful to the President of the United States. That means name calling, personal jibes, and/or belittling the President. If your goal in this conversation is to win, you could resort to these low and ineffective tactics. In fact, this behavior often leads to breakups. It goes from political discussions to personal attacks, all for the sake of winning an "argument." Let President Trump win in the short term.

A good therapeutic approach you can use when you're trying to find peace is to look for positives and what you two can agree on. Finding common ground will help both of you gain perspective and will certainly lift your spirits. From there, you'll naturally start looking through President Trump's eyes with a goal to find positivity in opposition. In other words, you'll give us renewed hope for the First Couple.

Don't go to sleep with politics on your mind. If it's ten o'clock at night, and you're starting a heated conversation, try to put a stop to it quick. It's never a good idea to engage in a heated discussion before bed. We have enough to think about before we close our eyes, as it's a common time for emotions to run high and tumultuous thoughts to consume us. Let's not add to it with politics at a time when we need to snuggle and love on one another. The bedroom should be a sanctuary—not a podium.

If none of these work for you, I recommend couples therapy. An unbiased therapist might be able to point out the positives for you and even ask the right questions needed to find common, respectful ground. After all is said and done, you will come out either stronger or more aware of what your limits (or "deal breakers") are. It's too early in your strained relationship for the division to be too wide. Although I'd never ask you to compromise your feelings, morals, or values in a way that makes you uncomfortable. It's about recognizing what is and is not a boundary and whether you're willing to cross it.

If it's not a "deal breaker" that you're dealing with, keep in mind that your love should mean more than any particular political disagreement. After all, you aren't running against each other in life; you're supposed to be running with each other. You may be on separate platforms, but you're still in this race together. Keep acting like it!

Hoping for everything good,

Ms. Priscilla Purity
Love and Relationships Expert

Is There Really Such a Thing as Work/ Life Balance?

Dear Mrs. Trump,

Please ask yourself, "Is there really such a thing as work/ life balance?" It seems as though you both are spending too much time at your jobs. For 40 hours a week you spend time away from the President and Barron. Out in the world, it is tempting to give too much attention to your aides, other First Ladies and, God forbid, other presidents, emperors, and prime ministers.

When you finally get home, if Barron is there, you focus on him. When that's been done, does the President receive your attention? And then, are you taking care of yourself?

While I could go on and on about how we give ourselves very little "me time," I would like to first focus on your personal interactions with President Trump and how work can be an obstacle to your much-needed intimacy. When your work follows you home, it can impact the Trump family unit as a whole, but it starts with the relationship at the head of the family.

Work and relationships are so demanding and require a lot of energy. When work receives your full attention, your relationship with your husband suffers. There will be many difficult times when it comes down to choosing whether to finish a task or to go home and be with the President. It's a hard choice, but life is full of them.

Please keep in perspective that family and relationships require nurturing and when neglected, everyone suffers (even work, ironically). On the other hand, if missing that meeting causes a national crisis, try to work with President Trump to make up for lost time. Mrs. Trump, communicate clearly that your decisions here are for the good of the family and will benefit them in a big way.

You two need to communicate, plan, and schedule—together. First, set expectations with the President so he knows what's important to you. Birthdays, holidays,

Grandparents Day at school, and family vacations—all of these things can be scheduled ahead of time. Prioritize them, and make sure your aides know that you must take the appropriate time off. Communicate with your husband kindly and humbly when discussing the special occasions you still may have to miss. Express what you need from Mr. Trump in support of your work. He needs to show understanding, flexibility, and encouragement. And then, understand when your partner says you're taking too much of his time. Just let him go without you. No hard feelings!

Mrs. Trump, feel free to speak about your dreams, goals, and tasks that are leading you down your current career path. If you succeed, it will be good for all the Trumps.

Always remember, birthdays and special occasions don't happen all the time, but regulated time together is just as important. Have a weekly ritual with the President such as game night, movie night, or watching cable TV together. This helps you designate time each week without the stress of quickly having to adjust to interruptions during your special time.

When you walk up the White House stairs, you're home. Be intentional when you're with the President. Think of it like this: put in the same effort with him that the Commander in Chief would for President Macron. Do your best for your biggest client. Carve out the time for activities with the same dedication as you would have for a major presentation.

An interesting way to dedicate the right attention to the Leader of the Free World is by meshing your two worlds. By inviting your partner to work events, you're combining the two parts of your world, making the President feel included, loved, and a part of your life outside the White House.

Never be narcissistic, and ultimately, make sure that both of you are compromising equally. Balance is crucial. That means working together to make plans, while still showing understanding when things fall apart.

Always good wishes,

Priscilla Purity
Love and Relationships Coach

Staying Healthy Together

Dear First Lady,

As I was thumbing through *AARP Magazine* this month, I noticed how centered the magazine was on certain aspects of health. It got me thinking about how easy it can be once out of the honeymoon phase to drift into personal complacency and end up in diminished health. When demands get out of hand, it seems that there's no time to live a healthy life. As a result, we can all let exercise and healthy eating fall to the wayside. However, staying healthy for yourself is also staying healthy for the President—and your relationship. Personal and relationship morale increases when you feel good, and confidence goes way up too. Here are some ways you both can increase your health as individuals and partners without it being a total drag.

It's obvious you take your workouts more seriously than Mr. Trump, but just as a reminder, you can work together with your husband to kick bad habits. We all have them. Tell him there's no shame here. Whether it's Big Macs or KFC he can't get enough of, or you tend to go straight to bed when you go upstairs in the White House, there are some habits that we fall into that might need regulating. It's most important at this point to help each other moderate them. Work together to call attention to particular habits in a loving, caring way. Say to the President, "Honey, you seem so tired and exhausted when you get home. I hate to see you like this. Are you not getting enough sleep?" Or "Have you tried dark chocolate? I hear it's healthier and good for your eyes!" These are some ways to call attention to the core of what you're saying: you care about him and his health.

Something I have found to be successful in helping couples eat healthier is cooking together. Get the President up and moving. Instead of going from President Lincoln's desk to the upstairs easy chair, make sure there's some movement in between—and a home-cooked, healthy meal at the end of his day as a special treat. Heck! You can plan the meal together! Presidents like to be seen, and shopping for groceries together is good optics.

Let the White House kitchen staff have the night off. Then hop in there and create something delicious and healthy as a couple. You might also notice that while cooking you may get talkative. It becomes easier to open up about your day or issues you're going through. It also brings to mind fun things that happened, such as a press gaggle or working on your Be Best program. Instead of cooking alone and letting your thoughts wander, you get to express yourself, which might spur some really good conversation.

Mrs. Trump, talking about your insecurities is not easy, nor is it fun! Honestly, even acknowledging that you have insecurities is tough. And for the President, it may be impossible. To get healthier, you both have to talk about the things you are insecure about, whether it's certain parts of your body or how he is seen by others. Communicate. Because without communication, neither of you can gain support for those insecurities. You both have needs, but you can't know what those are if you aren't open about them.

I just know you can be extra creative with date ideas. Hiking, trail walking, biking, swimming, anything outdoors and active are great options for a date. These are all available to our First Couple if the Secret Service is willing to go along with the idea. Even simply going to the Rose Garden to see the flowers or walking up and down the North Lawn steps—if it's getting the President up and moving, it's a good choice. If he's up for it, you can even work out together, forming a team that works off of each other for support, accountability, and a fun, unconventional workout routine. There are plenty of duo workouts in genres like yoga, Pilates, and high intensity training.

The most important thing in all of this is to be an encourager first and foremost—not a bully. Remember that it's not about changing Mr. Trump. It's about supporting him.

Wishing you health and happiness,

Priscilla Purity
Personal Coach

Being Friends with His Ex(es)

Dear First Lady,

I know you really must admit, you're the third lady. But don't let that discourage you. Men, like wine, most often get better with age. So my advice is to settle into the Ex-Wives Club and get close with your counterparts.

Understand, there is a fine line that follows after a break up. Your husband has been there many times. He's likely to have experienced periods of vulnerability, loneliness, and longing—vulnerability to falling into codependent habits, loneliness from being newly single, and longing for familiarity with someone close to him. This fine line originates from his wanting to remain friends with his exes and girlfriends, helping him cope with those feelings of codependency, loneliness, and longing. My advice on this is complicated because I believe friendship with exes is possible. However, there are limitations and conditions to consider for the sake of everyone's emotional health and wellbeing.

Help your husband understand that it is ideal for ex-couples to remain cordial and get along—not as ex-lovers but as people who respect each other's differences and separate lives. Meaning, he should have no lingering hostility. At the least, I suggest (if possible) help him find some common, peaceful ground on the things he might need closure on. From there, you can help him keep those friendships intact.

At the same time, getting along with his exes and being best friends with them are two different things. In this case, you're not likely hanging out with Ivanka or Marla every weekend nor catching a movie with either one on a primetime Saturday night. It would be easy to favor one over the other, I see. Ivanka could serve you well, as a wise older woman, but Marla would probably be a better "gal pal." So a simple and friendly check-in every now and then is innocent, and running into either one of them in public shouldn't be a terrible and awkward encounter. Just be kind and get along, while moving on.

The best way to keep a healthy mindset toward all of the President's exes is to not mentally write off these women's new lovers or partners either. It's easy to think, "No one could possibly be better than my husband." But don't let yourself think this way. This mindset breeds jealousy, unhealthy comparisons, and makes you bitter—affecting your ability to be optimistic about their new relationships. Remember that things ended with the President and his exes for a reason; it was probably some fault of all the parties involved. Therefore, don't get into a competition with the President, the exes, or their friends. These people should not have any control over how or whether you move on. That's only for you to decide.

The best way to do this is by letting go. Easier said than done, right? This is when the truth is hard to swallow. There is a lot to accept here: first, accept that you're third. Before you can maintain a healthy friendship with these women, you must move on mentally. Ultimately, let go of what was and look forward to new friendships.

Once you are able to let go of these old ghosts, start looking forward to the potential of your own relationship. It's okay to look back fondly. But by looking forward happily, you find yourself respecting the past much more and by default become more positive about your future with our Chief Executive. This attitude makes friendship with the old girls easier and healthier.

Good mental health requires closing your mind to cascades of blonde hair and trysts in bed with your mate. Don't let your imagination of other women with your bridegroom ruin your zest for sex. Just be happy that other women want what you have and never forget "the third time is the charm."

In Friendship,

Priscilla Purity
Mental Health Counselor

Moving in the White House—Do's and Don'ts

Dear First Lady,

I wrote this latest letter to you on the eve of your Inauguration. But would you believe—I forgot to send it! Still, it has some poignant truths in it that I still want to share with you. Here goes:

Having numerous roommates, whether it's people you know or not, is hard. You have to be considerate of others in your personal space. There are pros and cons to living in a gilded fishbowl, and I'm here to help put the odds in Mrs. Trump's favor.

First, before jumping in and merging all your residences, including 1600 Pennsylvania Avenue, make sure you and your husband both set clear expectations. One of the main causes of breakups and divorce is not having enough together time. So, from the start, give yourselves something to work with, and divide your time evenly or however you as a couple find fair.

Something we all underestimate when we're single is our alone time. When you're married, you always want to be with your spouse. Well, when you move in the White House, you live and work in the same house. You can see your husband almost any time you choose. It is very important that in your relationship, you do not lose your identity or sense of self. Continue developing yourself independent of the Commander in Chief. Having some space from one another is healthy. When you come back together after a few solitary hours of reading or posting on Twitter, it's refreshing, and you more appreciate sharing time.

As I have advised you before, it is so important to maintain the friendship in your relationship. Because when you start to see the less glamorous parts of Donald Trump, or the more human parts (and vice versa), it's a little harder to maintain the honeymoon phase. Rather, the relationship becomes more hard work, and that's okay. Relationships are hard. Don't believe otherwise. But that's what makes true love, true love at its finest. So, work on your friendship—the everlasting part of a relationship. Talk. Talk. Talk. Play. Play. Play. Work together.

When you move in the People's House, you'll probably notice your date nights start to fade into the abyss. You start telling each other little lies. For example, one of you may think, "We see each other every day, right? Why do we need to go to a restaurant when we can have dinner in front of the TV?" Well, that's not special. Your relationship will still take courting and romance. Never forget that you are with this man romantically; don't let the romance die. Don't let the Chief of Staff prevent your intentional date night on Wednesday nights. If it's something you're putting in effort for and planning for, then it will be something to look forward to where both of you can see each other in a different, more informal light.

Understand that there will be annoyances you find in one another, and these are not meant to be deal breakers. Only you can see some of President Trump's most astonishing hidden flaws and unique eccentricities. My dear, you have them too. So, give him a break, and try not to hyper focus on his quirks. Instead, embrace him. Laugh at him. If it's something directly affecting you negatively, like certain serious red flags, the next time you're on Air Force One together on a long haul trip you can talk about it. It might be something he can or wants to change. But in the end, if it's small, silly, and just part of who he is, let it be, and grow yourself into acceptance.

If you two are fighting, try to keep it upstairs and out of the East and West Wings. Every couple has a fight. But you two may be one of the "lucky" couples who don't really fight, or maybe you just fight very little. This is good, but if you as a couple have never had a fight over something, well... get ready. Living in the White House can bring out things in both of you that you wouldn't expect. It can be liberating and part of coupling in public, but having a healthy discourse at some point before settling in the big house is a healthy part of that process. It's important to know how each of you handles conflict before getting in such close semi-permanent quarters in front of the entire world.

When you're at home, it can be easy to default to looking at your phones while you're in the same room. This is fine, but when it becomes the norm, and you're realizing that you're talking less and less, try to limit your screen time for the sake of face time with the President. Be with each other intentionally, even if it is just at home doing the same-ol'-same-ol'. Sharing in these leisure moments together is special, even if it's low key.

Lastly, be kind to one another and enjoy this getting-to-know-the-American people process. Living in the White House can be enlightening and exciting. Do it as healthily as you can.

All the best,

Priscilla Purity
Lifestyle Coach

Double Dating
Do's and Don'ts

Dear Madame First Lady,

Have you ever heard of a thing called a "couples crush"? It's when you find yourself in the rare instance of liking both members of the double date couple sitting across from you (and vice versa). It seems you recently experienced a "couples crush" (as did many American women) when the French president and hottie Emmanuel Macron visited the White House. So often when you and the President go on a double date or state dinner, one of you doesn't like someone in the other couple. I bet it's really hard, for instance, to enjoy Angela Merkel's hubby. This can be frustrating, I'm sure. Dates alone with the President are great and often some of the best ones, but every now and then, a double date is mandatory.

International double dates offer even more to you as the First Couple: new experiences, perspectives, and opportunities that you wouldn't otherwise have. For example, I would think that bowling could be fun with the Japanese Prime Minister, but even more fun with a group of United Nations friends. Game night might work well with someone as youthful as Kim Jong-un. Heat things up with some friendly competition and allow some healthy interaction between dignitaries. If that sounds too intense, just plan on popping open some good wine and cooking Beef Wellington with Charles and Camilla!

During a double date, it must be fun to see the President in a slightly new light. It's almost like watching a movie you've seen before with someone who hasn't seen it. You're seeing Mr. Trump through someone else's eyes, which can be refreshing. Think about it; you may be used to seeing him one-one-one, without much of a glimpse into the social part of his life.

Now, in a double date environment, there are some downsides to be aware of. Watching England's prime minister, Theresa May, flash a smile across the table at something President Trump said on a double date might stir up your jealousy. And if that handsome Canadian devil Justin Trudeau needs to slip out for an important phone call during the date, be patient with him. Control your emotions. Be careful not to get too competitive or take sides too aggressively. This can cause bickering, jealousy, and some bitter vibes to permeate. Just be yourselves, be kind, and both be on your best behavior—unless the occasion calls for something a little rowdier.

Another downside to double dates will be the lack of intimacy because you and the President do need to limit your PDA, as it can make the other couple uncomfortable. That is, unless you all have an unspoken agreement that such intimacy around each other is fine. Beware especially of the Obamas—their charm is contagious. Don't be surprised if you and Mr. Trump experience increased intimacy after a double date with those two. Being out with others, seeing each other through different lenses, can be a great way to spice things up and specifically renew your flirting. Even at weddings and funerals. A great "after-date-night" might be just the reward you and the President need.

Double date compatibility is important. Sometimes, you will like one person in the couple and dislike—maybe severely—the other. What do you do if you or the President truly can't stand to be around him or her? Simple. Talk about this with your significant other. Things that bother you about that person, maybe they bother the President too. Ask each other important questions like, "Is it worth not hanging out with them separately?" or "Should we just stop hanging out with them at all?" Dinner with Attorney General Jeff Sessions, for example, would need this kind of discussion ahead of time.

Most important is deciding whether or not a couple is toxic to be around. The Clintons are an obvious example. If you don't have a good time with them, or you walk away unhappy with the evening, or feeling negative, keep that in mind as you figure out what you want to do. It just might be worth it to drop them from your Twitter or Facebook accounts altogether.

Now, when it comes to behavior on a double date, be sure to stay off your phones as much as possible. Keep the President engaged in meaningful conversation and ask questions of interest to the other couple. This is when you find common grounds for further conversation and developing the relationship. Don't downplay what's going on in your life, but it isn't the time for you to dump any of your personal relationship issues on the table. And when it comes time for the bill, I think the State Department should pay.

My last bit of advice? If you find THAT couple, the couple you have the most fun with and feel the most compatible with—who you like equally—don't let them go. And hope they like you too, or at least that they're really good at pretending they do!

Yours sincerely,

Priscilla Purity

Certified Dating Expert

Signs You're about to Get Dumped

Dear Mrs. Trump,

A relationship coming to an end is never a fun experience. It's one of the most painful things we can go through. Ms. Priscilla knows what she's talking about here, dear. But what makes it even more painful is when we don't see it coming. I've been there, done that. I know how it hurts, and now I know the signs of an upcoming breakup. Although they may be slightly different for everyone, I'm going to share some of the more common signs with you now so you'll be prepared for the unthinkable.

The first sign comes in the dreadful form of social media. Of course. If, in the early days of your relationship, he put up a photo of both of you as his Facebook profile picture only to put one up of only himself now, it could mean the President is having thoughts of breaking up. This is always especially true if the independent photo of him is a "sexy" or attractive picture. If so, he is likely preparing to find other relationships. I know this hurts to hear, but it's better coming from me than finding out the next time you're surfing online or Mrs. Pence is holding the line for you.

"Phubbing" is the next sign. I'll give more detail on this phenomenon in a later letter, but "phubbing" is when your mate ignores you while looking at his phone. This can happen with friends, family, or romantic relationships. In the relationship setting, if the President is doing this more often than usual (because it happens often anyway), it could be for a variety of reasons. It might be that he is becoming bored (harsh, I know), or trolling for another relationship. If he seems uninterested in your day and instead looks at his cellphone during moments that should be just about you two, the relationship is likely in trouble. Here's the real test: if you confront him about it and he becomes defensive or simply ignores you, you should prepare for the inevitable.

Another tell-tale sign that the First Couple's relationship

is heading in a bad direction is if he avoids making long term plans with you and instead takes long weekends at Camp David (which could be code for somewhere else, let's say, the Playboy Mansion). Making plans means planning for the future, and if he is avoiding doing that, it could mean that he doesn't see you in his future. This is the moment to have a sit-down, as you cannot wait around to find out if there's a fourth Mrs. Trump waiting in the wings.

We've all heard it again and again: communication is the key to a good relationship. Well, it's common knowledge because it's true. Once that line of communication is interrupted or even severed, that's when fights, misunderstandings, distance, and damage happen. If communication has died down, it's crucial that you try to regain it. However, if he's not talking and acts more interested in Fox News than in your day, your life, and your concerns, then it could be a sign that the distance is coming between you—on purpose.

Along the same lines, if you two still communicate but only when you're fighting, you may want to evaluate what you're fighting about. Toward the end of a relationship, the fights become less and less productive and rather focus on smaller, insignificant things. This means there's resentment built up somewhere, or one of you is realizing that the other's personality just isn't compatible with yours.

If the fights are left unresolved, then it's a sign that neither of you is really willing to fix them. In order to grow from the experience of a fight, you both must tackle the issues early and head-on. Solutions are crucial at this time, but if the President or you are not willing to try, your reluctance may be for a reason.

There are other signs, such as fewer moments of intimacy, whether it's just saying "I love you" or physical touch, or if he seems happier when he isn't with you. Watch the Cialis bottle. If the contents are vanishing, yet President Trump is leaving on his pajama bottoms with you, check the Lincoln bedroom for evidence of someone tempting another future lawsuit. Again, I know that's harsh, but it's important to keep your eyes open when you're starting to have doubts about how Mr. Trump is feeling. Not only do you deserve more than just these "signs," but you also deserve to be with a person who loves you and treats you right. So, the earlier you can see the signs, the quicker you can try to solve the issues—or not—and then, the sooner you can move on to better things.

With sympathy,

Priscilla Purity

Talking about Your Significant Other, to Others

Dear Melania,

Most recently, I wrote you about the importance of communication with Mr. Trump, but what about the importance of communicating *about* the President to others? No need to fret. Priscilla knows exactly how you should talk about the President to other people, such as friends, family, and world leaders.

Mrs. Trump, we've all been there. Let's say you had a fight or disagreement with the President the night before. Something really upset you and you needed to talk about it.

This is normal, but it can turn sour. While there are times when we all need to vent properly to friends, that doesn't mean unloading every negative thing that happens, every time it happens, on anyone who will listen. Not only is that a slippery slope toward a habit, but it can exacerbate negative emotions and create a big mess for you and the President.

If you need to talk about something, the first rule to abide by is never to choose the press or Vladimir Putin. It seems obvious, but don't choose a random group or even a group you think you can trust. Designate one or two people you know will not judge you and who love you. Having an audience who listens without judgment is a healthy environment for a productive talk. If someone has this approach while listening to you, they're much more likely to offer good advice and support that will leave you feeling fulfilled and in a positive mindset to approach your partner later.

Next: there's a difference between bashing and venting. If you truly love your husband, try to remember that when you're talking about him. It will help you keep a healthy perspective, instead of driving your negativity into something habit-forming and honestly, just mean. Bad-mouthing President Trump is a bad idea and a bad sign of marital problems. It breeds more negativity and will leave you feeling guilty afterward—instead of relieved or fulfilled. Be sure you're talking in a healthy, productive way; something good should come of it, even if it's a simple feeling of relief.

Balance. Balance. Balance. You may fully trust your friend or mother to listen and not judge, but keep in mind that they are human. They love you and want to protect you. If the negative heavily outweighs the positive, they will begin to wonder, "Why are you with Donald Trump at all?" This is the point when it's too late to explain all the positive moments you have together. It'll come out defensive and scrambled. Be sure that while you vent sometimes, you also often talk about the good times like when President Trump surprised you with flowers. Let your friends in on the good because when the bad happens, they can help gauge advice with a healthy perspective on the relationship as it truly is.

Lastly, if you are feeling resentful about something, and healthy venting still isn't helping, then it's a definite sign that you need to bring this issue to the President. He needs to know that this problem is driving some division between you and that you're not getting relief or peace from simply seeking advice from a friend.

Also, if the other things you vent about are causing you emotional distress, even if it goes away after a healthy talk with a friend, the President may need to know about it, as it could be recurring. Always talk to him; be open and honest in a kind, loving way. Sometimes resolution may come after you speak to a friend, and that's okay. Just remember that he is also in this relationship and deserves to know if he is upsetting you or damaging the relationship in any way, even if it's something small.

Yours truly,

Priscilla Purity

In Divorce, Think about the Adult (Trump) Children

Dearest Melania,

Divorce isn't easy for anyone involved. It would be especially hard on both of you, your young son, friends, and other family. What about the adult Trump children whose parents have already split up once? It's a different ballgame, and I think there needs to be more insight for parents who are splitting up and how they can approach it with their kids who aren't kids anymore.

I'm leaving little Barron out of it for now as he is a child. But Don Jr., Eric, Tiffany, and Ivanka have lived all their lives knowing their family unit one particular way, and if something rattles that, their whole foundation is rocked. All of your traditions, memories, the way things were or used to be, will now be different again. That's hard. In a way, it's like grieving a death. The people are still there, but everything in your life that "was" is changing. Many negative things happen as a result—a sort of chain reaction that's tough for the Trump kids to avoid.

When going through a divorce with older kids, first try to think about the way you'll tell them. Will you do it together, or will it be announced through social media or the press secretary? Will you tell the whole story? Will the President be honest with them? Will you make it clear how much you love them and that the divorce doesn't change that fact? Make sure that before the conversation happens you and the President have a civilized discussion about what you both agree on revealing, depending on the nature of the situation.

Then, think about the physical and logistical changes that will take place. Will you get the penthouse at Trump Tower? If so, do your best to ease that transition. Maybe keep many of the gold leaf furnishings intact, for everyone's sake. Certain traditions may have to fade, but if there are any that can remain, try to keep them. You created these traditions for the Trumps; maintain some of them, civilly.

And if you can't do so, make it a priority to create new ones that are just as meaningful.

Unfortunately, with divorce there is often one person in the marriage who leaves much less financially well-off. Depending on your pre-nup, this might be you. Sweet Melania, you might struggle financially. Sometimes the responsibility falls onto the adult children to step in to help, because it's not the other parent's "job" anymore to take care of the other parent. This is probably not going to be the situation in the Trump family. It is likely you'll only see your step-children on Facebook or New York's infamous gossip outlet, Page Six.

As adult kids, things are much different in the divorce conversation. The Trump heirs could hear the President refer to you in a negative light, which can be tough. In that case, you have to see your step-children as humans, with very human and adult flaws. The problem comes when these kids try to pin you as the villain and pull you into the narrative in an unhealthy and unfair way.

Constant negativity from the Trumps, incessant bad-mouthing, showing resentment on their sleeves—it's all unhealthy for you and their relationship with them. Eventually, the Trumps could start thinking about it from your perspective, causing a fresh wave of resentment toward their dad. This is highly unlikely, however. So, stay strong. Keep it positive, mature, and healthy—for the kids' sake. And yours. If the Trump kids ask for details, and you're okay disclosing the answers, do it appropriately and respectfully of Donald Trump, not only as your ex but as your kids' other parent, whom they love.

Mrs. Trump, one more thing. If you notice young Barron becoming distant, don't give up. Show him that even though you're starting a new chapter of your life, he is the most important part of it. In fact, show your son how much you want him to be a part of the story forever.

All the Best,

Priscilla Purity

Dating as a Mother

My dear Melania,

It hurts me personally to give you this advice. But in case you decide living with Donald is impossible, please understand one thing: dating is hard, even for the former First Lady. Just look at Jackie. She was forced to take that smarmy little Greek man. Being a parent is hard enough. Try doing both dating and motherhood! Each role is full of stress, but for some people both must be done. Here are some tips to help you get back in the game after separating but also to guard your heart while it's at its most vulnerable.

Re-entering the dating world is scary, especially since you've been out of it for a long time. My advice may sound a little contradictory, but just hear me out. Don't rush in, and don't stay out of the game for too long (if you can help it). As for that first piece of advice, it's so important for you as a newly separated woman to be careful and not rush into anything too soon and too seriously. You'll be incredibly vulnerable and in need of affection and attention, but this is the most crucial time for you to really find yourself and figure out who you are independent of Donald. That way, you will become happy with yourself without relying on anyone else for your source of joy.

Forcing yourself to stay single for the sake of your son, or just because you're afraid of dating, is likely not a good time to stay alone. If you feel ready, but something is holding you back, try to put yourself out there and see if that hesitation goes away after a date or two. Dating is not always just about meeting someone; it's about conquering a fear that may have been there for a long time as a result of your previous "failed" relationships. In other words, don't let the past determine your future—you've got this, girl.

You may feel you should only date one person at a time. I say, feel free to date a few people at a time, but be candid about that option with those you are dating. It's a good way for you to compare and contrast desirable and undesirable traits. It's even more important to date before you jump right back in and commit again to one person.

Depending on their attitudes, be careful introducing your date to your kids and family too soon. It might be wiser to ride out the dating relationship for a bit before taking it to that level. If the children get used to the person being around, it can really hurt them if the relationship ends. Wait until things are more serious, stable, and a sure thing before bringing anyone else into the equation.

Your children should be mentioned on the first date. Now, that does not by any means mean that you should talk about your kids the whole time. If Donald's kids are an issue right off the bat for your new man, so be it. You should be dating people who are in the right mindset—the kind you need. Speaking of mindset: be sure that the man you're dating is also in the right mind space to date. Maybe your new man just got out of a marriage or a relationship in the last month. Are you sure you want to put your heart on the line for someone that vulnerable? Think it over.

I also suggest not dating any other presidents. I realize Putin is single and does have a good body for a short, older man, but the Russian women are gorgeous and stiff competition. You don't need this aggravation.

Dating can be hard to find time for, but it's just like working out; you have to invest and make time for yourself and your health. Utilize all means of help from your parents and friends for covering the bases at home with young Barron's soccer practices or music lessons and take that night out you've been needing—with someone potentially really great!

Melania, ultimately, you should enjoy yourself. Dating isn't meant to be miserable, although there are always going to be a few miserable dates here and there. Hey, it makes a good story if nothing else! Accept that this isn't easy for anyone, but it's meant to be an experiment—a fun one—so let yourself have a good time in the process. Don't put so much pressure on yourself to the point that you aren't yourself. You deserve this opportunity for new love. Go get it!

Wishing you every happiness,

Priscilla P.

Improving Intimacy in Your Relationship

Dear Friend,

We are friends, aren't we? I hope so because "intimacy" can be a touchy subject for some (pun intended). Often, when the topic of intimacy comes up, you or the President might shell-up and shut down. If your relationship lacks intimacy, it's easy not to bring it up. One of you may not want to discuss it, while the other desperately needs to talk. I promise you, there are ways to improve the intimacy in your relationship, whether it's emotional, physical, or both. It just takes an open mind, a devoted heart, and a willingness to talk about it—no matter how taboo.

Intimacy comes in all forms, and it's pretty crucial to a healthy relationship. However, a big disconnect happens when you realize that intimacy is quite fragile and that it can fade over time through the different seasons of your life. The important thing to realize here is that this is normal. Do not—and I repeat, do not—let this reality shatter your relationship with Mr. Trump. Why? Because that fiery passion isn't going to be there forever, and that doesn't make it bad; it just makes it different. Understanding that fact from the start is vital, but it's just as important to understand that in order to keep some of the passion alive, you may have to try harder over time. And that's okay.

Intimacy isn't just about sex, though I can suggest many ways to improve that part of your relationship, too. I have found that non-sexual practices are the key to improving the sexual aspect of one's relationship. For example, taking a walk with Donald at sunset with phones off can increase an authentic connection between you—a connection that you can so subtly and easily get lost. Giving each other massages before bed can be another way to show Donald you love his body, you love touching him, and you want him to feel good. It can stop there, but you may both go to bed lovingly, or something more could take place. Who knows? But in the end, it's all about allowing your walls to come down for a bit and letting each other in.

To improve your intimacy, get to know what your partner values in that area. Is it sharing quality time? Words of affirmation? Does the President just need to hold your hand throughout the day? Maybe he needs to be held before bed. Really, think over what the President needs, specifically, and then think about what you need. Once you realize what is important to you, communicate that need and work together in making those efforts.

A more modern way of staying connected and making sure the President knows you're thinking of him is by sending flirtatious text messages—with or without selfies. Be sure you do this on his private cell phone. Vladimir does not need to pry! Other ways of increasing that closeness is by intentionally making out as you did at the beginning of your relationship (you'd be surprised how this can shock the President and be a great re-connector). I know I'm beating this drum again but cook together. This often leads to dancing or arms wrapped around someone's waist. I mean, come on. Food always puts Donald in a good mood. Utilize that for your benefit.

In the end, however, if you do not love yourself the right way, it's incredibly hard to recognize and accept the right love from the Commander in Chief. You may be mean to yourself about your physical appearance, or maybe you don't think you're very funny. Work on crushing these false beliefs. You're beautiful, and I thought the irony behind launching your anti-bullying campaign right after the President's Twitter rant was an absolute hoot! Very funny. Melania, work on truly having an intimate relationship with yourself so that you can feel deserving of the love and affection around you. In that same way, you can give out the right kind of love to Mr. Trump.

Yours,

Priscilla Purity

Divorce Proof
Your Relationship

Dear Melania,

As we all know, the nature of marriage has changed drastically the last few decades. In fact (and unfortunately), 50 percent of marriages are ending in divorce. Although there are many reasons for divorce, some marriage practices will help keep your union strong.

The first rule is pretty simple, and yet it doesn't happen very often: marry a person you enjoy being with. You see, a friend is a longer term relationship than a lover. Choose someone with whom you can be your complete self; that means both the pretty and the gritty parts. In the end, you and Donald need to love each other's company, because at the core, it's who you both are when the world isn't looking that matters most.

The second rule is to develop real trust in each other. The President or you may have spent years building up walls, tackling rejection, or just not finding the right one, so it's easy to begin to lose trust in each other. It's hard, once you do find someone who treats you and loves you right, to break down those walls. But you must. Be an open book. Be transparent. No secrets. This actually leads me to the third rule.

It is essential that you leave the line of communication open both ways, always. How else will you know what the President is thinking? And if he is thinking something negative, how can you help turn it into a positive if you don't even know it exists? Talk often and early when a problem is raising its head. Compromise, but don't compromise your principles. Simply listen, and keep an open mind, heart, and ears.

I also want to suggest that you develop a couple's identity. This doesn't mean that you lose your personal identity in any way; it just means that you are sharing your life and yourself with another person. Show that you're proud of that. Let the world know you're a couple. Hold hands when descending the stairs on Air Force one. Touch each other; share a public hug on the White House lawn; and have a mindset that you're "in it together." You're a team—not competing.

There is a huge part of this that people don't put enough weight on: the commitment part. Through all the painful, ugly, and not-so-glamorous parts of marriage, be determined to stay. When it feels the easiest to leave, that's when you shouldn't. And don't ever threaten to leave or file for divorce when these problems arise. It can become a habit, and eventually, it could come true.

Trust me, dear Melania, I know that none of this is easy, but I do know it's possible.

Your friend,

Priscilla

How to Accept that Your Spouse Has Someone New

♥

Dear Melania,

I've been thinking about my last letter to you. Should you decide to break up with Donald, please know that breakups are never easy. The pain doesn't just stop after the first week. Even once you've mostly healed, the hurt can come back with reminders, memories, or songs. One of the most hurtful hurdles post-breakup, however, is realizing that Mr. Trump will find someone new. The wound is reopened, and it comes with a lot of other emotions: jealousy, loneliness, curiosity, and maybe even the feeling of betrayal. So, really, it's more than just one hurdle; it's several hurdles lining the track before you get to the finish line.

In my experience, I've learned a few things about myself in those painful stages of a break up. Sweetie, have I done some things wrong! Now I can look back and see how I could've done better, treated myself kinder, and healed quicker. So I want to share some of that wisdom with you this week.

The majority of the process to healing through a breakup is coming to full acceptance of a few things. First, recognize that you will indeed be overly curious about his love life, in addition to being hurt and upset, either overtly, covertly, or both. Understanding and accepting that knowledge will prepare you for the emotions to come.

It's always hard to believe there will be another woman or women. But don't let yourself suspect that they may be better than you. Just because your ex is with someone else doesn't mean that someone else is better than you; it means they're different than you. Do your absolute best to avoid comparing yourself to the new person. You have your own strengths, uniqueness, and weaknesses; so will the new women. The truth is, though, their strengths don't and shouldn't matter to you.

Now, the next piece of advice may be the hardest, especially in today's world. It's been proven that social media can impact your mental health. Stalking the President online is incredibly common, but don't do it. Also, don't stalk his new love interest as well. This is a bad move for your health, and you should take measures, however hard, to keep this from happening. I suggest blocking the President and his new lovers on all social media platforms. Even though it's tough taking that first step, you'll thank yourself later for taking away the temptation to torture yourself scrolling through their lives.

Anger often leads to bad decisions, and when you find out your ex has moved on, it may spark some of those angry feelings. In moments of emotional rage, you may feel the urge to give in and call the President to express that anger; do not do this if you can help it. Telling him off will only hurt you more. More importantly, never go to *The New York Times* and criticize the new love interest or Mr. Trump, as it shows insecurity and won't make you feel better. Trust me.

You ought to also take care of yourself physically. Overeating and undereating will only hurt you, put you in a worse mood, and threaten an already mentally vulnerable state of mind. The same goes for drinking too much or using other substances to mask pain or push down uncomfortable feelings. The best thing to do is to let nature and time do all of the hard work for you; just try to sit back and allow it.

Take nature walks, do yoga, meditate, read, or take up a new hobby. Learn and practice relaxation techniques and think positively.

Lastly, remember not to let the urgent feeling that you must find someone else right away consume you. Rebounding is a dangerous game and can sink you lower into loneliness, complications, and confusion. Your emotions, rightfully so, will be imbalanced during this time, and they need to rest and reset without the dependence on and the noise of someone else.

We all want to feel that we are the best our ex will ever find and that he will somehow remain celibate after our relationship. Of course, this is not realistic for your husband and sets you up for disappointment and further pain. Recognize that you and the President had a unique time together, yet something just didn't work, and that's okay. This is commonplace, and you shouldn't carry guilt or experience depression when you pick up the latest rag magazine at the drugstore and see your ex moving on. Try healthily to let it go, remembering the good times, with your eyes looking ahead for a new beginning.

Focusing on the positive,

Priscilla Purity

Sleep and Relationships

Dear Melania,

There are a few things in life that can severely affect our mood: being angrily hungry ("hangry" I think they call it), stressed out, or exhausted. Exhaustion in particular, can have a big effect on your relationship with your husband—from sleep problems, to a lack of snuggling, to snoring. This week, I'd like to share some little-known facts about the connection between sleep and relationships.

Lack of sleep—less than seven hours per night—leads to low energy, fatigue, and daytime sleepiness. Although it's not good for Mr. Trump to be seen taking an afternoon nap in the Oval Office, the effect on his libido without that nap can be much worse. All of us who sleep poorly display more negative emotions and behavior, and because of this, we can get into arguments more easily. We don't resolve conflicts as quickly or effectively as we would if we got enough sleep. I feel compelled to say that the President at times displays actions of a man who is sleep deprived.

It may be difficult to get your husband to change his ways, but you should not be the one who lets lack of sleep get in the way of connecting with your partner. You don't want to be hostile or irritable toward him, so prioritize your own health for the health of the relationship.

Snoring is an issue many relationships struggle with. I'm not sure if the President snores, and I cannot think that you might be a mouth breather, but if either of you are the offender, know that snoring often creates tiredness, frustration, and resentment between you. It can even cause couples to sleep in separate bedrooms, so it's not just hard on you, but on Mr. Trump also. As snoring interrupts sleep, it wakes up the mind, which makes it very difficult to fall back into a deep sleep. This leads to impairment in judgment and irritability in the waking hours. Surprisingly, even crazy social media messages and strange words like "covfefe" have been known to be sent out during these bouts of insomnia.

It's common to do nothing about snoring, especially because most couples usually don't mention this problem in marriage counseling. This could be due to embarrassment or maybe neither spouse sees it as a cause of relationship issues. But as a savvy marriage counselor myself for many years, I've made it a habit to delve into this matter. I suggest you try the following things to address the issue with the President because I have a sneaking suspicion that you know what I'm talking about.

First, you must talk to the President about it. If you are the guilty party, let him know that your snoring bothers you just as much as it may bother him and that it's out of your control. If he is the one who snores, try to say reassuring things to him. Most people are self-conscious about their snoring. Second, seek medical help by visiting your doctor or going to a local D.C. sleep clinic. Ear plugs are great for a temporary fix. Another way to drown out the noise is by keeping a sound machine on—maybe one with rain or jungle sound effects.

Another issue that affects sleep is temperature differences. Our body temperature is regulated by the hypothalamus in our brain, and many things can affect it: medication, illness, muscle mass (the fitter we are, the higher our body temperature), menopause, and/or circulation problems. To address your varying body temps, consider using separate blankets or sleeping in a bigger bed. If the White House bed is too small, you can ask for donations to get a new one. (Remember, Nancy Reagan did this back in the day to get new chinaware.) You can have a down blanket, while President Trump may be beside you in the buff. Now I'm getting too personal, dear, but the point is that we all have our own comfort levels, which fluctuate from night to day.

Cuddling in bed can be lovely for the two of you. In fact, I recommend cuddling several times a week, but do not feel pressured to fall asleep this way. Sometimes, it's best to just start out cuddling and then go your own separate ways. The President may not enjoy cuddling at all, but he might enjoy his freedom as he rests. In that case, you may need a dual-zoned bed to achieve satisfying temperature preferences.

The President may prefer to retire to bed early, while you like to go to bed late at night. It's possible that one of you prefers to watch CNN before bed, and the other wants complete silence. My advice would be to go to bed at different times, which is really no big deal. Just be sure to say goodnight to each other.

In the end, we sleep about one third of our lives, so let's make the First Bedroom as pleasant as possible.

Sweet dreams,

Priscilla Purity

Phubbing, A New Way of Ignoring

Dear Melania,

Do I even need to tell you that modern-day dating and relationships are completely different than they were decades ago? This is mostly due to one particular reason: technology. Technology poses good and bad things for our relationships and daily encounters; not only does it help create connections, but it can easily help you stay in touch with family and friends in Russia and Slovenia.

On the other hand, it has created quite the distraction in a lot ways. Social media can give you reasons to not communicate in person with President Trump, and checking your social media accounts are often a default action for when you feel awkward or bored. Therefore, it may hinder you from learning how to just "be in a moment" and keep you from being confident when eating alone at a restaurant, for example.

On average, we check our cell phones 150 times a day. I won't go into all the ways technology has affected each of our daily lives and relationships, but one in particular has to do with a phenomenon I introduced you to earlier called "phubbing." Funny word, huh?

Put simply, phubbing is just ignoring the person you are with. It's also called, "Phone Partner Snubbing." In other words, it means your phone might be more interesting than the President and that you'd rather focus on your smartphone than pay attention to your husband.

Yes, President Trump is guilty of this also, and phubbing can send negative and hurtful messages such as: "You're not that interesting," or "You're not that important," or even "I could be talking to someone else right now." This can cause the other person to feel discounted and not valuable, which then creates conflict. In its essence, phubbing is a major hindrance to communication, which is just a stepping stone to worse problems.

When there's not good communication, people can

grow distant, fight more, and even suffer intimately. Such alienation can also cause trust issues, as one person remains in constant wonder about what the other person may be saying about them to the other person on the phone.

This stuff is no "phunny" business. (Ha!) Phubbing is in the top four reasons for divorce in this country, along with money, sex, and kids. It's important for lovers like yourselves to become more self-aware and make some changes, even if it goes against his second nature of screen addiction.

Before pulling out your phone, be thoughtful enough to ask the President before you do it. That gives Mr. Trump comfort in knowing that you are aware of his feelings and the potential of your actions bothering him.

Also, be open to Mr. Trump also phubbing every now and then. Have an agreement that it's okay to do it occasionally, and be sure to keep yourself from taking it personally when he does.

Ultimately, you both need to get out of your heads and out of the virtual world at your fingertips just for a minute to see each other. You and the President don't have a lot of time on this earth. Don't waste the moments you could be looking into each other's eyes, hearing his voice, and connecting on a deeper level than his Twitter account.

That's all for now,

Priscilla

Building Confidence as You Age

Dearest Melania,

"Getting Older" is a title or tag that we both dread. However, it is possible (though maybe not so easy) to go through this process with style and grace. Our attitude plays a huge role in our advancing years, with three things in particular being of utmost importance: confidence, positive self-esteem, and realism. Building and maintaining these confidence-based traits involves practicing the following mindset.

My first rule for aging gracefully is to embrace each day

with optimism and curiosity. What's in store for you today? If you have a lonely schedule, change your calendar. Fill it with things you enjoy—or things to challenge yourself. Look for interesting activities such as talks or museums. Heck, why not start a lunch group with the Senate wives? Get out of the White House every day, if possible, even if it's for a short while. Be open-minded when creating your schedule, and look for activities that will improve you as a person. Doing so will definitely add to your self-esteem in an organic way.

Although social media and television can be fun pastimes, it has also been proven that these can cause depression, boredom, apathy, and numbness. Lingering on a photo or post from your old boyfriend somewhere out there beyond the doors of the White House often leads to us comparisons. This can make you feel even more lonely. Yes, social media can connect you, but it can also discourage you.

Don't grow older by being around only old people. Stay involved with youthful acquaintances and friends. This doesn't mean to hang around solely those who are younger than you, although that can help; it's about being around people who still live young. Take Paul Ryan—that man looks and acts like a kid! Individuals who still have a zeal for life such as Elizabeth Warren will fuel your drive for living. Having friends of different ages also gives you fresh perspectives, which can be hopeful and inspiring.

Dwelling on your ailments can be quite the downer. Try to keep your health conversations or comments to a minimum and focus on your positive attributes. A lot of times as people age, they may become less optimistic and will want to share their burdens with you. It's easy to forget that others have their own burdens. You want them to come to you as their healthy escape, just as you want to go to them for the same reason. So don't over burden them with your woes. Of course, be polite if others engage in their difficulties. The next time Mitch McConnell brings up his double chin, smile and listen. But try not to encourage his sad stories. Always give a positive, uplifting spin, or simply listen and don't add too much to it.

As for style, you have it! And you can keep it! Even if your husband's legal bills become overwhelming, don't punish yourself by keeping the same wardrobe forever. You're still allowed to shop and have new and stylish things. Go for contemporary—nothing too youthful or immature. With the whole world watching your every move, it's easy to flash a little leg. Don't do it! Stay with styles that empower you, bring out your beauty, and make you feel good. Go for classical items with a colorful, fun twist. That's always been a good approach for Ms. Purity. Same goes for the hair; nothing ages you like a bad hairdo. As we both age, we will have to be careful with our hair. It might get too long and can pull things down (you know what I mean). I personally have to work on avoiding a Dolly Partonesque big-hair debacle.

Something unfortunate about today's society is the pressure women feel to be flawless, even as they age. This is especially true for you as First Lady. Perfection is impossible, so why even try to cover everything up? Try not to cake on makeup. Keep it more subtle so it simply enhances your look—not overpowers it. A natural way of trying to prolong youthfulness is by keeping up your exercise routine. Exercise not only keeps you physically healthy, but it also puts you in a good mood. The same goes for eating well, even on long haul flights to Japan to see your husband's favorite prime minister. I encourage you to experiment with your food, not flinching when you're offered the delicacy of tuna eyeballs in Japan or fried spider in Cambodia.

Don't let the President discourage you in these areas. And while we're on that subject, I wanted to share a surprising and somewhat creepy fact about how people who are together for years may start looking alike. I don't know if you were aware of this phenomenon when you married the President, but you don't have to accept this. At a minimum, I'd advise not adopting his hair color—yellow is such a difficult color.

Most important, though, is having a flexible attitude. For so long, we've been the adults and we've done things certain ways, but it's time to break that mold. "Live and let live" and "seek to understand" are wonderful age reducers.

Must run—there's a sale going on today!

In friendship,

Prissy

The White House Can Be Awkward & Uncomfortable

Dear First Lady,

This letter might make you squirm in discomfort for a minute, but hang in there with me because it has to do with a topic we need to cover. In the era of the #MeToo movement, we need to address something I know that many people encounter in their day-to-day: awkward work incidents. This can include you, our First Lady. A congressman might hit on you or pull you in for a hug at awkward moments. Or let's say a CIA agent or aide is guilty of invading your personal space.

Each of us has different levels of comfort. I know many people who, in these situations, will simply ignore how uncomfortable they feel or give the offender the benefit of the doubt. If doing this is your preferred route and you're at peace with it, that's fine. But if you're forcing yourself to deal with a situation like those mentioned above or worse, that's a problem. No one should be made to feel uncomfortable in the workplace where we spend about half our lives.

Trust me, as a female growing up during a time when there was no #MeToo movement in sight, I've seen and been through my fair share. That's why I'm sitting down to write you about the best approaches to dealing with, getting out of, and preventing these situations. Please share this letter with the President. He is susceptible also.

First things first. You should report any incident that makes you uncomfortable to the White House Human Resources department. That's their job—to make the workplace a safe and secure environment. You should feel unthreatened as you do your work in the East Wing. Remember, any information you share is confidential at the People's House. So don't hesitate to report a problem. You never know. What's happening to you could be happening to others in the workplace, and it's not just women who are victims. Everyone is at risk for these situations. So, if I had to choose one route, I'd say stand up and say something. But you do it in your own way, the safest of which is speaking to someone in charge.

Now, you may hear a common response to these incidents along the lines of: "Well, dress more modestly and maybe it wouldn't happen." I call BS on this. I always wear high-collared blouses, and men still leer at my bosom. Neither should you as the First Lady have to change how you're dressing just to "stop something from happening to you." If you are ever told this, ignore it. It's not the right answer. People will do what they want, regardless of what you wear.

If someone at work hits on you or makes you feel uncomfortable, you are absolutely allowed to say boldly, "I'm uncomfortable" or "No, thank you" or "No, this is very inappropriate, and I would like you to leave me alone." If there are multiple instances, action must be taken by that big strong man, Chief of Staff John Kelly. Be sure to record every occurrence, as many of your colleagues have done, noting times, dates, and details.

The case gets more serious when someone touches you inappropriately, especially your private parts. If any world leader, member of Congress, or advisor does anything from touching your arm too many times or too intimately, to standing too close in proximity, you are allowed to openly show your discomfort. Move away or state it out loud, "You are too close," or "Please don't touch me." This should get peoples' attention.

If it's just friendly hugs by coworkers, make sure you make it clear to your peers if hugging is uncomfortable to you. Honestly, if you're an avid hugger, please keep in mind that many people aren't—especially at work. Keep it professional until you know for a fact that that person is hug-friendly. Otherwise, respect each other's personal space, even if you mean well.

If something threatening has happened and you have reported it, stay aware and hope the FBI follows up, or at least is surveilling the perpetrator. Check in every now and then with the Attorney General if you're curious.

Lastly, stay aware of how you're feeling. If it's distracting to even have this person nearby, don't accept meetings or social invitations when this person is in attendance. And if you are finding that you're feeling emotions of guilt or shame, talk about that with someone trustworthy, perhaps your mother. You should not feel anything close to guilt or shame for something another person did. It isn't fair for anyone to be comfortable every day, after having made you uncomfortable. An abuser should not make you feel guilty. It's not on you; it's on the victimizer.

Stay strong, stand up, and make a difference for you and the entire #MeToo movement.

Sister power!

Prissy

How Do YOU Experience Love?

Dear Melania,

I want you to know that men and women think differently, so we also tend to experience love differently. Now, this may not be an airtight theory, but I do think there's a lot of truth to it. It's wrong to assume that men don't experience emotions to the degree you do. By the same token, it's also a mistaken belief that women have "too many" emotions.

You may or may not be aware that there's a theory floating about that you are more logically-minded than Mr. Trump, while he is more irrational and makes decisions based solely on emotion. Misconceptions develop concerning you and the President in part because we ALL experience love differently—including the two of you.

Melania, it seems that because of the culture we live in, men's expression of emotions, including the President, has often been stifled, but it doesn't mean they don't have feelings. Society is changing, thank goodness, and encouraging healthy emotional expression—instead of making us hold it in. Various books and articles have emerged proving that men tend to feel loved when they are shown respect. It's the opposite for women: we feel respected when we are shown love.

I can definitely see where this principle could apply to the First Couple. Respect and love are interchangeable. To feel loved, you should absolutely feel respected. To feel respected, there is a certain overarching love that comes into play, as well as admiration. It all comes down to how you and Donald each individually interpret love.

Let's define the word, "respect." Sometimes, the word is interpreted as someone respecting an authority figure because they have some special knowledge or power. However, in the context of a healthy relationship, we're talking about partners who are treated equally. It means we trust our partner's decisions and believe in their judgment.

If the President disagrees with you, he should value your opinions and feelings and discuss it fairly. It's not about controlling each other. It's about truly loving each other enough to give the other equal standing and the exact consideration you'd want for yourself. It's also about feeling free to love fully and be loved fully. My advice is that the President needs to know what you value most and what your expectations are. Just make sure you're incorporating both love and respect into your relationship equally.

Yours truly,

Priscilla Purity

Finding Love after Fifty

Dear Sweet Friend,

This is a personal story I want to share with you. Married for 69 years, after a short illness my dad passed at 90 years old. My mom, five years younger, was a remarkable caregiver during his confinement. Several hours after Dad's funeral, their friends and relatives left and my elderly mother and I were alone. I admitted how concerned I was about her living by herself. Smiling, she looked me in the eye and said one of the most loving statements that only those who have spent more than half of their lives married can say. The conversation happened like this:

"Mother, what will you do now that Dad's gone?"

"I'll be fine. I plan to go to Wal-Mart every day."

Flabbergasted, I asked, "What? Why Wal-Mart? What do you need there?"

She smiled again. "I need a walker," she said.

"A walker? Really..." I was now totally perplexed. She seemed to walk fine for her advanced years.

Then my mother continued, "I need a man to be my escort and keep me from getting bored."

In shock, I vacillated between anger and shock. Another man so soon? I couldn't breathe. Then my mother uttered the words that have brought me peace and love eternally for both of my parents. She said, "Your dad always told me, 'I don't want you either alone or lonely. Find a friend as soon as you can and live life.'"

Fifteen years ago, online dating was out of the question for a rural 86-year-old woman. But my mom was clever. She determined that the local Wal-Mart was a ready bastion of semi-retired male greeters who enjoyed people and would be ideal for a date. She could select her new beau undercover while pretending to shop.

Melania, my purpose for sharing this story is manifold:

1. **There is no magic age for dating.** Older relationships can be simply wonderful.
2. **There is no perfect timeframe for mourning a death or loss of a loved one.** If you are happiest when you are busy and social, only you should decide when you re-enter the relationship world.
3. **Reentering the dating world or deciding it is not for you is your decision.** Whatever you decide, it should be supported, not criticized, by your children, friends, or relatives.

I am a later dater myself, and I've written many articles on love and relationships. Goodness, I've spoken to hundreds of singles at this point. Whether someone is never married, divorced, or widowed, entering or reentering the relationship world is frightening, exhilarating, and exhausting.

The President has a very stressful job, and let's face it, he doesn't appear to be a pillar of health. You may be a widow someday. If so, my wish for you is to find your own "walker." You have lots of options: single heads of state, corporate business moguls…the list goes on and on.

Time is ticking. Let's get busy!

Priscilla Purity

What to Do on Those "Off" Days

Dear Melania,

I know you have those days when everything just feels... off. Your communication might be awkward; you might be overthinking things; maybe your temper is a little more sensitive. Not every day is perfect—at work, at home, or in your social circles. Interactions aren't always going to go your way.

I'm here to tell you that it's okay. We all get in our heads at some point and are unable to pull ourselves out. And the harder part to accept is that it will inevitably happen.

You can't make every day at the White House perfect, so just accept right now that you will, in fact, have off days, especially when you're interacting with the President and his Cabinet. I know Chief Kelly can be a hard a**, but you'll be okay. People may comment on how quiet you are. Or they may overhear you bickering with Donald. Maybe you're distracted by the President's Twitter feed that day. A lot of things could be the cause, and it could be something you need to talk about eventually. But sometimes it's just that day's mojo. You can get through it, and I'll be here to show you how.

Sometimes, it takes sleep to break the curse. You might need to just rest, clear your mind, and reboot before further interactions with anyone. If you're stuck in your head and you can't turn your mind off—and it's influencing how you are acting with people—shut your eyes and rest. Sleep is always a good go-to. (Just don't make it your only go-to.)

Other days, you might need to just wind down a little with a glass of wine and a chick flick in the White House media room. Then, talk about it with the President. Come together once you've had your mental rest from the day. Just because you need a little space doesn't mean something's wrong. Just don't stay upstairs in Mar-a-Lago too long; that's when people suspect something deeper is going on.

A lot of people find working out to be a great way to put the mind at rest by exhausting the body. Exercise releases endorphins that could put you in a better mood and, as a result, a better mindset to interact and get through the day. If you're dealing with a tough day in the East Wing, and you're just not vibing with your staff, get away from them. Show your independence and go to a D.C. pub. This way you'll be around people, but ones that you may never see again.

If you're feeling off in a solemn way, have a healthy cry. That doesn't mean have a mental breakdown in the Situation Room. Your severely off days could be symptoms of a bigger issue, so pay attention to what your urges are. If you're feeling a cleansing cry coming on, go for it. But if you're feeling the weight of the world on your shoulders and you fall into a spiraling, ruminating sob, something is happening mentally or hormonally that needs attention.

At the end of the day, maybe all you need is a hug from Donald. No words, no hashing things out, no diving into the things bothering you—just human contact with the person you love. That hug, in a way, can disrupt the turmoil you've had in your mind all day. It quiets it and reminds you that you're there for each other—not always to solve the day's awkwardness, but rather just to ease it. Later on, you may want to talk about your day and even laugh about it, which will definitely bring you closer and put things in perspective.

Above all, if you're going through something tough, that is a good time to lean on the President. Remember the Chief Executive is the most powerful man in the world. His shoulders are broad. It just depends on what you're needing for your mental cleanse. Mrs. Trump, you're not alone in this. The whole United States feels a little low every now and then. Don't be so hard on yourself. Get through it, rely on those who love you, and give yourself some breathing room.

After all, tomorrow is a new day.

Devotedly,

Priscilla Purity

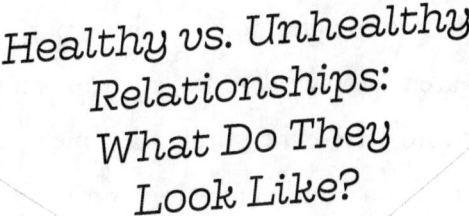

Healthy vs. Unhealthy Relationships: What Do They Look Like?

Dear Girlfriend,

Things aren't always black and white in relationships. There's a lot of give-and-take, compromise, learning curves, and mistakes made—and none of this is easy. Loving Donald can help you develop and improve, as it highlights some weaknesses you may have and need to work on. Acknowledging those things about yourself can be positive and lead to incredible character growth, but it must happen in a healthy way.

There are times, however, when all we see are our own

weaknesses, and in turn, we feel ashamed. It's easy to blame yourself when the President calls you a name you don't like. Love can blind you from knowing when your weaknesses (maybe they aren't even weaknesses) are being exploited and used against you. That's when things become unhealthy. In fact, that's when you should know it isn't really love.

That's what I want to write about today.

A healthy relationship is built on one very important thing: communication. When you feel like you can't communicate, or you're afraid to say certain things to the President, something is happening either internally or in the relationship. It's okay to feel nervous or embarrassed to say certain things, but once you do, it's important that you're met with encouragement to always express your feelings. If Mr. Trump meets you with hostility or beratement, something is definitely wrong.

Feeling as though you have to hide anything from the President is bad, and the reasons why you feel that way need to be looked at. I've known people who have been afraid to even eat certain things in front of their partners for fear that they will receive harsh words about how terrible their diet is, with other insults mixed in. This cannot happen; it's bullying. Similarly, if you bring up problems and your husband immediately dismisses them, shuts them down, and becomes defensive, it's bad news. Why would anyone bully someone they love? Because he doesn't value your feelings. If he responds with, "I don't know why you always have to complain..." or "You're making me feel terrible..." or "I guess I should spend the night downtown in the Trump International Hotel..." these are not acceptable responses to legitimate relationship discussions.

The President shouldn't manipulate and twist your words. If he turns an argument around on you and makes you feel as if your feelings are unreasonable or even "crazy," seriously consider the future of your relationship. Responses similar to, "What are you talking about? I never did that... You're the one who's overreacting..." are unacceptable. This kind of manipulation (lying to make someone doubt their own perceptions) is called gaslighting, and it is a particularly vile form of abuse.

A good relationship is push-and-pull. Meaning, some days the President should support you, whether it's financially, emotionally, or maybe even physically, and other days it will be vice versa. A constant back-and-forth flow of support without begrudging each other when you need that support is key.

Lastly, not having aligned goals in life will make for a bad relationship. There are big ones, such as children, marriage, money, and lifestyle, that people often never discuss because there's a narrative often pushed that "true love can overcome anything." However, true love means sticking together through thick and thin, and you do often need to be on similar life paths in order to do that.

So if you aren't fully happy in your current relationship; if you feel like you aren't quite yourself when you're with them; or if you feel as though you're "walking on eggshells," take a look at your relationship. It might be time to either consider counseling or move on. And there's nothing wrong with that, by the way. Of course, it's possible that things are going very well and you're both truly and authentically happy. I hope for the latter.

If you ever need to talk, I'm always available to you.

With love,

Prissy

When You're Down, Talk It Out

Dearest Melania,

I can see it in your eyes. You seem a little depressed. Here's my advice. The world can be a difficult place. You see it every day on the news: a shooting, discrimination, children caught on the South Texas border. And although you did wear that darling green jacket with the proclamation, "I Really Don't Care, Do You?" I think fashionistas should shut up. I know you didn't mean that! Think of all the difficult things that happen in your personal life: Don's fluctuating moods, another manicure, pesky aides, and that damn TV which makes all of us look heavier than we really are—the list goes on. In your day-to-day, it can be a lot to handle, especially alone.

Often, however, we all keep it in. When there's a lot weighing on us, we generally do not talk about it. But we show it. We get distracted or lost in thought and are easily irritable or quiet in conversation. Why don't we talk about what makes us sad? Common reasons have to do with the fear of bringing the mood down. Or maybe you're already having a bad day and you don't want to make it worse. Perhaps you think, "Sarah Sanders is going through a lot with the press. I don't want to bother her with my issues even more." It feels almost like an emotional trap, I imagine. There is a fine balance here that must be attained in order for you to be healthy and have a good marriage.

Anyone experiencing sadness or going through depression can make the relationship feel like an insecurity, and insecurities are incredibly hard to talk about. But you must talk with the President, because you are allowed to feel what you feel.

My first rule about communicating your sadness with Donald is to be intentional. Being intentional about taking care of yourself and him sometimes means talking about the hard stuff, poking him to talk about it, or deciding to not talk about it for a bit and having fun or finding peace instead. The goal here is to be aware of the issue and work together—sometimes to discuss it and sometimes to take a break from it. And that's okay. Doing those things on purpose and together, instead of Mr. Trump's deciding alone not to talk about it, is important.

Science even says so. There was a recent study by Berkeley (I love these fun schools) called The Sharing Effect that suggests that simply knowing our partner is going through the same emotional situation makes us feel better than we would if we had experienced it alone. I think, to a degree, we are the emotions we experience. Our relationships are, in part, about sharing who we are with another person. Girlfriend, you have to be able to share who you are in a relationship, even if it temporarily causes Donald to have negative feelings.

Often, those negative feelings come from things he can't control. That alone is frustrating, but sharing can help you cope. Also, you shouldn't shut down, head upstairs, and stay completely uninformed about the negative things going on in the world. You also need to separate the time you spend thinking about your relationship and time you spend taking care of just you!

Sharing isn't about fixing, my dear. It's about sympathy

and empathy, which are relationship builders that also build trust and intimacy. It's about learning what the President needs and how you can respond to those needs. I'd like to share a perfect example of this, which took place in my little friend Amanda's life just recently. She wrote me:

> "We went on a trip to Disney World, the happiest place on earth, and even there I was having an occasional panic attack of anxiety and existential dread. *What am I doing here? What are we all doing here? Wasting time and money? How fake this all feels? Why can't I enjoy it? I must be some terrible, ungrateful monster if I can't even enjoy a vacation we worked so hard to pay for.* But then, I did the thing I've learned works best. I talked about it. I grew up in a family that didn't discuss emotion. It wasn't that we were emotionless. To the contrary, my family and I fought often in my childhood. But there was never a discussion as to why. This caused problems for me with relationships in my early adulthood, and so, through painful trial-and-error, I came to the conclusion that open communication is always a good thing.
>
> "So, I told my boyfriend how I was feeling:

scared, angry with myself, disgusted with myself, frustrated, confused, sad. But as the feelings poured out, and I looked at his intently listening face, I felt another emotion: comfort. I felt gratefulness seep into me like a warm balm. This person is my partner, I thought, and he's listening to me and trying to help me feel better. I was letting the depression out like cleaning a wound, and it was helping. We talked about why I might feel that way (was I tired/hot/hungry/overwhelmed?). What could we do to make it better? He said that it was okay that I felt this way if I acknowledged it. It was only a problem if I let it control me. Through removing myself for a moment and discussing my feelings, I was controlling it instead. It worked. I still felt a little anxiety, but it was muffled, like sound behind glass. I could function and I could continue to enjoy my day, with my partner's hand in mine."

Isn't this just an optimal communication between partners?

Now, on the other end of the spectrum, sharing emotions is necessary, but a person who isn't a licensed therapist like myself shouldn't be treated as one. If you have trouble processing your own emotions beyond what can be handled by you and the President, you need extra help. And again, that's okay. Just talk...and talk to me!

Hugs and kisses!

Priscilla

Women's Changing Roles in History

Dear Melania,

As our First Female Leader, and such an inspiring role model, I wanted to point out that you are now a part of our history. A lot has changed over time for women. More specifically, much has changed in the relationship and family realm for women. From the traditional stay-at-home mom who wasn't allowed to write checks, women can now be CEOs and politicians and take charge of their own finances and their love lives. I feel that it is vital for President Trump to understand that he doesn't have to be so macho.

Societal pressures for women to look perfect and meet certain beauty standards in order to be "desirable" are still high today. But these standards were much more widely enforced years ago in America. They still might be in Slovenia. Not only were wives meant to bear and raise children, they were expected to cook, clean, serve, sacrifice in their relationships—all while maintaining youth and beauty. Thank God you have help in the White House and natural beauty.

Being a Slovenian, you need to understand that since the 60s and 70s, American women have been greatly liberated from these expectations. Instead of the primary cultural focus being on how to conform to a certain body type for the sake of feeling wanted and loved, it's more about embracing our bodies as they are. Being healthy is the goal, and that is becoming the new "attractive," as it should. Michelle Obama was definitely not a stick.

Just like Ivanka, moms aren't the sole and primary keepers of the house. However, there is still some work to be done. While more men are taking household initiative and women are working full time jobs, women still tend to take on the roles of keeping the house, planning family events, bill paying, and errand running. I mean, really, can you see Jared Kushner cleaning a bathroom? Mothers are still the ones staying at home with their kids who are sick and are the ones serving on school boards and clubs and attending field trips.

On the upside, there are many more husbands who are cooking, grocery shopping, and taking on some of the tasks traditionally expected of wives. Now that more women are working jobs just as time-consuming and energy-draining as their male counterparts, they are starting to divide up the day-to-day responsibilities equally. The male role 100 years ago was quite different, and now that it's evolving, it's benefiting them and women alike. Back then, the man was expected to work outside of the home, support the family completely and financially, and keep his emotions to himself while doing it. Society did not allow men weakness then. I think Mr. Trump might want to tap into his softer side.

Today's husbands and male partners (I hope you don't mind me mentioning LGBT) are able to feel more emotionally available to their significant others. They're not under the false impression that they should have no part in the raising of their children. This transformation has helped the marriage and family construct in general. More emotional availability and involvement in the kids' lives means healthier and happier families (and wives). It means less pressure on the wives and husbands to meet their culturally inflicted stereotypes. You might also consider speaking to Chief Kelly about this. He appears so hard-nosed on TV.

Sigh. I digress.

No matter what, all relationships are different, multi-layered, and complicated. Some wives choose to take on both the traditional and modern roles, though this may become overwhelming. As long as it's a willing decision to take on a certain role, rather than doing something based on what history has told us, you'll have the ability to live happily ever after. My opinion? Use history as a lesson. Gain wisdom from it. Be liberated by it. And that Omarosa, don't you agree, is something else.

Cheers, dearie,

Priscilla

A lover of history and strong women, just like you

Love in
Bloom

Dear Melania,

Ah, spring is in the air, and so is love. Washington D.C. is so dreary in the winter, no? Now is the time to get yourselves back outside and in the sunshine. Apart from the bit of rain I've had at my house, the weather has been glorious. That's what spurred my thinking about the perfect springtime couple ideas to share with you.

When I think of spring romance, I think of flowers, strolling outdoors, and refreshing food—and my suggestions incorporate all of the above. One of my favorites is the D.C.

Farmers Market. Not only can you both take a stroll and be around nature's best produce and fun novelty shops, but the President can take a break to enjoy a few cookies in one of the Farmers Market eateries. While you're there, buy some ingredients to cook together later to keep the date going!

I'm not sure if there is a well-known plant shop near the White House where you can find the best East Coast plants and flowers. I love this date idea because nature makes people happy, and you can even buy a small plant as a memento of the date. I'm thinking maybe you can place a spring daisy in the Oval Office on the President's desk.

If you two feel frisky, go on a Yoga in the Park or Yoga on the Bridge date. They have classes for free at parks all over D.C. Two things to keep in mind. First, if the President has stiff joints, yoga doesn't have to be strenuous; it's about movement that's right for both of you. Second, exercise releases endorphins, which might put you both in an even healthier mindset toward each other. As a plus, if you're at a park with food trucks, you've got the "lunch" or "dinner" part of your time covered. After a time like this, it's easy to feel more confident, productive, and free.

The city's arboretum is another way to be in nature without being out in the Virginia wilderness. There are romantic spots for photos, water fountains where you can sit and talk, and shady trees under which to picnic. Sometimes, your arboretum will even have live music or events going on to set the perfect natural scene.

Imagine being with the President on an outdoor porch, sipping his Diet Coke and maybe sharing a fresh Caesar salad. Of course, in peak summer heat the sun can be a bit much, but in the spring you and the President can spend some lovely evenings on a nice breezy patio at the White House. This setting could be perfect to spark a little romance between you two. Being outside gives you space to talk, while not leaving you in complete silence where the conversational pressure gets to be too much.

Lastly, don't feel as if you have to be outside constantly. Enjoy the outdoors without forcing yourself outside all day. Take a drive through the rural Blue Ridge Mountains— the Secret Service will enjoy it! It will give you a great opportunity to really talk to one another and enjoy the beautiful views along the way.

Don't forget, my dear, that the cherry blossoms will be blooming then. You can enjoy the smell and visual appeal of walking through the many trees as you stroll hand in hand with your beloved. What could be more romantic than that?

Wishing you happiness!

Priscilla Purity

Back to the Basics of Friendship

Dear Melly,

It's probably time for you and the President to get back to the basics of friendship. All relationships start differently. Some start out as friends, while others become romantic almost immediately. My guess is that Donald started kissing you as soon as he saw you! But at some point, there comes a time when friendship levels in a relationship are at their highest. This is a great part of any relationship: the friendship. It's when you can be your most raw, vulnerable, and trusting—aside from physical intimacy or attraction.

It takes a deep connection with someone to be friends with them genuinely. In my opinion, every relationship requires friendship, even yours and our Commander in Chief. Without it, things aren't exactly sustainable. At the end of the day, physical connection may dwindle slightly. What remains? Your emotional connection, your best friendship.

When you've been in a relationship for a long time, and yours is fairly long, your friendship can fade. How do you get it back? First, be honest with yourself. Relationships are hard. Period. When the friendship fades after a while, so do other parts of the relationship. You must be intentional and put in the effort to make it work, to get back to the core of who you are as the First Couple and as individuals.

Try to identify the things you used to do in your relationship that felt right. Did you used to express how you felt about him more often? The President loves cable news, and maybe you used to really value that about him. Have you said that lately? The same applies to other interests. Really believing in each other and valuing the things you each love make you more attracted to each other. Sometimes, it's delightfully shocking to hear your significant other affirm you. After a while of no words of affirmation or indication that they're interested in you, it can be a nice change to hear some praise and attention. For example, you might say to the President, "You're really improving your golf game. I'm so proud of you."

Being an adult can be such a drag, and working in the White House can be especially taxing. If you aren't careful, the nation's needs will consume you. Life will become about the mundane routine of "getting things done." My advice? Have fun again. How about you and the President letting loose? As I mentioned in another letter, take a walk to some food trucks, drop an ice cream cone on the ground, take an Uber to brunch, try something new together. Be spontaneous (without jumping out of a plane...unless that's your thing).

Along those same lines: laugh. Let yourselves laugh and experience the less serious parts of life. If you look for them, you will find them. Find a show to watch together, one that doesn't cause stress, or share some fun photographs in a book. Have discussions about them. Disagree, agree, just communicate. There are times when you might recall something that the President doesn't remember. Share it. It'll refresh his memory and impress him with your recall, while also making him realize that you do cherish times with him—even those as simple as that one moment of a memory. It meant something then; it means something now. Talking about the first years of Barron's life and all those happy memories can rekindle your love of being new parents.

Lastly, reminisce deeply. Often, when a relationship is struggling to get back to the basics of friendship, you'll hear the problem described as, "Our relationship feels flat," or "There's no spark left," or "Our relationship feels empty." Even couples who are on the brink of divorce can think back on certain memories and smile.

So, when things feel "empty" or "disconnected," reconnect by remembering. Get back to your foundation because it's still there. I promise, your feelings of friendship and closeness will come back. I know you both can "spice up" your relationship. You just have to try and try together.

Your BFF,

Priscilla

You're Splitting Up. Who Gets the Pet?

Dear One,

If you are both too stressed at your jobs, I have just the thing. You both need a pet. A pet is a must to lessen any problems with a split up, should that come up down the road. Be aware—the CDC National Center for Health Statistics reports there are more than 800,000 divorces each year in the United States. With that comes a whole other chain of events. Who gets custody of your son? Who gets the NYC apartment in Trump Tower? But one other question will become paramount with a new addition to the

First Family: Who will get the pet?

Around 63 percent of all US households, and most former U.S. Presidents, own pets (mostly dogs) according to the National Pet Owners Survey. Now, with so many divorces taking place, and the possibility of the first one by a sitting President, it's not hard to calculate the potential of there being many fights in the process of splitting up. I, for one, could not imagine having to fight for custody over my precious dogs. But if I absolutely had to, I would keep one rule in mind: the pets come first.

A dog would probably be good to both of you, love you unconditionally, and while you may not love the President anymore, the dog still would. That's worth considering. All of this is easier said than done, but it's worth putting into practice if you ever find yourself in this unfortunate situation.

While the Supreme Court may not recognize pets as family members, but rather as possessions, it's best to try to settle these things outside of Ruth Bader Ginsburg and her colleagues. Not to mention, it's absurdly expensive to fight for pet ownership. The next step is to consider all the pros and cons for your pet and outline these maturely between the two of you.

Sometimes your spouse may use your dog as a weapon

against you. Let's say you got a dog and had him the rest of the President's term in office. Consider first which of you the pet would have a stronger connection with or attachment to. If it's obvious, try to stay strong and accept this. From there, you can work out visitation in a civilized and loving way only if Mr. Trump wants to have joint custody. The other thing to consider is housing. Will you have a backyard? Will the President have more space in general because of the Rose Garden? Should the one with more space keep the pet until the other person gets a larger space? Until then, set up a civilized visitation schedule and revisit the decision later.

Often, when a couple separates and fights over a pet, they forget that they're single now. It isn't easy to take care of a pet while single. If you're having lunches at Bergdorf Goodman's, you're not going to want to cut that short to let the dog out. Consider that. Do you think you can even take on the responsibility of a dog, even if it's the cutest, smartest ever? Maybe the President will be retired by the time you get a pet. He'll have a more flexible schedule and can devote more time to the responsibilities of pet ownership. Like I said, the dog comes first. Always.

Now, one more thing about this "visitation" or "joint custody" thing. It doesn't have to be as terrible as it sounds. If you really don't want to see each other after a split but you want to see your pet, have a dog walker (or the President's butler) transfer your pet between homes. If you don't mind seeing each other, you could send a quick text: "Hey, it's your day to have Lucky. Come by whenever." If you've set up a schedule and/or signed on the dotted line to abide by it, then it shouldn't be an issue. In fact, this could come in handy if one of you has plans. Mr. Trump certainly can't get out of an overseas business trip to acquire a new hotel at the drop of a hat. It takes forethought.

Joint custody is shared responsibility. It means caring for the dog equally, like sharing the weight of vet trips and meds, but it also gives you the right to that leisure time with your beloved pet. The rule? Don't put all the difficult tasks on your ex and expect to get all the fun parts. Be fair. Share the weight; share the love.

In the end, your dog will become part of your family. Treat him or her with the love, care, and maturity they deserve. Even Ivanka and Jared might grow close to little Spot. Don't use the dog as a weapon; don't force him to live with the President if he doesn't want to. Do what's best for him. Otherwise, no one else will.

Sincerely,

Priscilla Purity

Signs of an Online Dating Scammer

Dear Melania,

God forbid if you divorce, but you must emotionally prepare yourself. You've been out of the dating game for decades, and maybe the President has also. It's imperative that you understand and be prepared for new dating trends. I want you to know, "The one true happiness in life is to love and to be loved." This quote by George Sands is so true. We all long to love and be loved. From birth to death, love is a basic need. But today's world has drastically complicated this search.

Divorcées and widows find in today's world that online dating is commonplace with 49 percent of dates, regardless of age, arranged through dating apps. What was mostly seen as taboo ten years ago is now wholly accepted and embraced. However, with all things positive comes a downside.

Dating scams are growing every day, and far too many of us looking for love are susceptible to being scammed. In fact, 15,000 complaints of online dating scams were reported to the FBI in 2015; that number was up by 2,500 or more in 2016. Even more disturbing is that $230 million was stolen primarily from women searching for love.

Be wary, my friend!

I'd like to devote this letter to some tips for recognizing the sleaziest of sleaze, an online dating scammer. How can you recognize these felons before you might be their next easy prey?

1. The scammer tries to establish a relationship with you quickly. In this situation, you must have the FBI research his background and photo online before caving in to his compliments.

2. The scammer quickly endears himself by flattery. Always know that "too perfect" is never perfect.

3. The scammer tries to gain your trust. In this case, be sure the FBI asks questions in different ways to catch him lying.

4. The scammer wants you all to himself, isolating you from your family and your friends. Be careful and always trust your friends and family to review his messages and give you honest opinions.

5. He never visits you in person but has a problem that only your money can fix. Big. Red. Flag. Never ever send any man money. Tell him no, and see if he goes away.

You'll be doing your sister "later daters" a favor by calling the FBI and reporting the louse before he tries his charms on another person. These are hard lessons in finding love, but anything that's worth doing is worth the effort and caution. Keep looking for love and keep your antenna up.

Remember, America's First Lady, you're worth it!

Toodles,

Priscilla Purity

A New Year, A New Love for Yourself

Dear Melania,

The New Year calls for many changes, some good and some not so good. New love, new responsibilities, maybe a new exercise routine—it's all in the realm of resolutions. Something I've noticed, however, is that many resolutions start off with the wrong intentions: meeting someone else's (Donald's) expectations. If you decide you want to find more love this year, you will start looking immediately. If you want to find a new initiative and give up on "Be Best," you will start focusing on the search. If you need a better exercise routine (you look fabulous), focus on social media posts, advertisements, and articles of society's hottest women for "motivation." Bear in mind that *The New York Times* is not always the best read. But it's important for you to start focusing on developing your self-love first.

How can you love someone or allow them to love you if you haven't committed to loving yourself from the start? Talk to Donald about this. I think he loves himself enough. How can you find a new commitment that will make you just as self-satisfied and happy, if you aren't sure exactly what that looks like? How can you change or implement an exercise routine without really focusing on why you're doing it? Is it because you want to feel better? Be healthier? Or just to look like Kim Kardashian so the world will love you? Although we all love you, it should be all about *you* loving you.

Each year, I choose to focus on the good and recommit to practices that worked for me in the previous year. I want to share those practices with you, dear friend, in case they resonate with you in your efforts to start the New Year by pampering yourself.

For years, yoga has been at the center of my mental and physical well-being. Not only is it a physical practice, but it always starts with what's important: internal growth and love. I do yoga three to four mornings every week, all year long. I'm sure there's a place in the White House you can stretch out. A simple stretch flow or more advanced poses help in relieving stress and promoting positive emotional feelings. It's a time that I intentionally set aside for myself— something we are not used to in this society. Turning off phones, devices, alerts, and notifications is a must for this time of calm. Don't let the White House staff interrupt your peaceful feeling.

Along similar lines, meditation is a significant practice for mental health. After having had cancer 28 years ago, I chose to implement meditation into my healing for the first 15 minutes of every day. I started this right after my surgery in 1989. It was and is a wonderful way to wake up slowly, be mindful of the direction of my thoughts, and enhance my peacefulness, even in not-so-peaceful times...and especially in not-so-peaceful times. I'm happy to share my innermost feelings with you, my friend, and hope you feel the same.

As for more physical health aspects of loving myself in life, I feed myself on a healthy and consistent level. I eat meals—small meals—five times a day. They are not always nutritious. (But that's also part of loving thyself. Indulge.) I start out with a small meal after yoga, lunch midday, a light snack in early afternoon, another around five in the evening, and then a last light meal later in the evening. These meals may be small, but they certainly enhance my energy, which is, truthfully, the whole point. You can do this. Instruct the chef to make nutritious snacks and meals for you and the President. Goodness knows he could stand to lose a few pounds.

Emotionally, I try to zero in on those areas that cause me trouble. For many, jealousy is a struggle. We all have at some point looked on social media and television (or just those around us) and envied what they look like, what they have, or maybe whom they are with. You should never envy Michelle Obama's arms. They're untouchable. Envy is toxic, which is why I've worked hard over the years to free myself from it. It can become a prison, so I refuse to lock myself inside those bars. Instead, I love myself by not allowing jealousy, and yet I accept and acknowledge that I have faults. I do not beat myself up or shame myself; I am human. Sometimes, I'm lazy and unmotivated. Sometimes, I'm in a bad mood. Regardless, I make it a habit to like myself and love myself through it—as I would hope others would. I feel that you have the fortitude to stay balanced even with Donald's outbursts and tweets.

Lastly, after you have found self-love, allow yourself to also love others. Look for the good, and you'll see the good in yourself.

Happy New Year, dear friend!

Priscilla xo

Breaking Up or Breaking the Bank?

Dear Friend,

Relationships aren't easy, and these days somewhere near 50 percent of marriages end in divorce. A main reason for this is finances. Either a couple is slightly incompatible in the financial area, or they are what I call "financial opposites" with completely clashing ideas on spending and saving. What's worse is when these incompatibilities fail to be communicated before marriage. Prior to walking down the aisle, a couple should at least discuss the big issues: money, children, and stepchildren. Did you and the President discuss these?

That's my first rule regarding relationships and finances today: talk money before marriage. I'm not sure of your situation financially. Many couples now have pre-nups. I always say that if you have already tied the knot and currently struggle with financial tension in the relationship, sit down and have a mature conversation.

That's rule number two. Be very clear with Mr. Trump what your spending patterns are, and don't be ashamed. If one of you tends to spend more and he spends nothing, each of you can actually help the other improve. After all, that's what relationships are all about. While you can help him loosen up and enjoy what he's earned, he might help relieve you by encouraging a little more frugality. These practices will help as you grow and will allow you a more prosperous future.

Next, set clear spending and saving goals together as a team. By matching up your goals and vision from the start, you leave less room for discrepancies, dysfunction, and disappointment later on. Not only that, but with an agreed-upon goal, you can both plan better for the future. Sadly, if any of the news media outlets are correct, he might have several lawsuits awaiting him once he leaves the White House. If there isn't miscellaneous spending happening constantly and harbored cash sitting around somewhere untouched, you'll both be on the same page and be better prepared.

Remember, it's just as important to plan realistically and agreeably. Compromise is essential. Meaning, a saver will have to spend a bit more, and the spender will have to practice restraint. Ultimately, be realistic for one another by perhaps getting some of your staff to do some unbiased research on organizing finances for proper budgeting.

However, even when you set realistic goals and compromise per one another's needs, problems will inevitably arise. When they do: Communicate. Communicate. Communicate. When you accidentally (or not accidentally) overspend, let the other know—not so you can argue, but so you can work together to adjust the budget accordingly. This will put each of you at ease, knowing that when problems come about, it's not the end of the world. And it's certainly not a relationship deal breaker.

No matter what, keep in mind that marriage is a partnership, and it needs to be fair and equal in every way. It can be complicated, tense, and even scary, but do your best to think of the person first, before thinking of their price tag. Money can be compromised on, but when there's too much or too little of it, there can be repercussions. A strong relationship will withstand these obstacles and maybe even come out better than before. Don't be part of that 50 percent.

In friendship and solidarity,

Priscilla Purity

Dating Now vs. Dating Then

Dear Melania,

If you ever choose to fly the gilded nest, there are just a few more things you need to know. Dating is different today than it was when you met Donald, however there is now a mix of generations from the spry Millennial to the seasoned Baby Boomer that connects our whole world.

Melania, one of the biggest differences between you and younger women has to do with the kind of technology you grew up with. The younger generation has almost always had the Internet and cell phones, which are highly utilized in the dating world today. Millennials tend to be in constant communication via texting, chat apps, and social media, while you and I went longer periods without communicating with our lovers.

While constant communication fosters a different relationship dynamic than in previous generations, there's definitely a certain dependency and expectation that comes from perpetual communication. Social media is a major modern avenue for that.

Social media has been around only a limited time, but it is now a huge staple of our society. What this means for dating is that young people have much more transparency in their dating prospects. They can easily look up someone's past jobs, education, relationships, cities they've lived in and more, unlike any generation before. We have access to social media as well, but our past history is generally a lot shorter, more professional, and is of course missing chunks of content from before the Internet's proliferation.

One of the downsides to social media is that much of what you see online is staged or made to look its absolute best, when the reality may be much less glamorous. This could mean that real, honest moments may be harder to come by because everyone is trying so hard to look their best online. You are not guilty of over-tweeting, and you could help the

President by guiding him to hold his tongue and his tweets like you do.

While younger people have technology and social media on their side, we older people tend to have more face-to-face experience and intimate knowledge in dating and relationships. Many of our prospects have been married, are divorced, and/or have been through a number of serious relationships. Because of these experiences, we tend to not waste time and cut right to the chase. Women our age typically don't sit around wondering, "Is he into me?" or "Is it going to work out?" Rather, we often look for companions with common interests and don't waste time with people who are aren't a good match.

In my experience, I've noticed that we often worry about someone's ability to look after themselves. More specifically, financial stability is important to this generation. Young people, on the other hand, are used to instability—both financially and emotionally. I think this is due to being early on in their professional careers, as well as this new "open dating" culture where many relationships are less committed and more casual. Although this can be freeing, it can sometimes translate into uncertainty within relationships.

Oh, look at the time. I'm afraid I've only scraped the surface of dating in today's world, as we could dive deeper into technology and varying relationship values between generations. But I'll save that for later. At the end of the day, even though our methods and definitions of dating are widely different, we are all still looking for the same things: love, companionship, and emotional fulfillment.

And that's what I wish for you, dear friend.

Yours truly,

Priscilla

How to Blow
Your First
Date

♥

Dear Melania,

Since you've had no time to write me back, I feel certain
that my letters have been helpful. But this may be my last
letter to you for a while. So, okay, Cinderella, if you ever
decide to re-enter the dating game, here's my final bits of
advice.

Jumping back into that world can be invigorating for you.
But you'll have some anxiety and anticipation. Anxiety
about what Americans think of you. And anticipation of
meeting someone new. The excitement may even have a

negative impact, as you suddenly become more concerned with your own flaws and may become blind to the flaws of your new friend. You may even look over the obvious, probably like you did with Donald's flaws.

Admit it. Thinking of a new man makes your heart flutter. You talk yourself down, then back up, and back down again and all around and into a frenzy. But have no fear; it's not unusual to be this nervous, especially for the first date. Just beware of the following sure-fire ways to flub the first date, and try to leave these dinner discussions at home.

1. **How your ex was so horrible.** Your date will know how many years you were married, but like most Americans, he may wonder why you stayed so long with the President. Watch your tongue here. It's not wise to harp on the past when you're trying to start fresh and new. Those conversations will come later. For now, it's about you and your date. Not the President.

2. **How Donald was a saint.** For the same reasons as above, make sure not to spend time discussing your ex and how wonderful he was. After all, why would you have left such a sainted sphere for the divorce court? Don't appear like a masochist in waiting.

3. **Your finances.** Donald may give you money, but the day may come when he is financing a younger woman. Either way, your new man will not want to hear of

your overdrawn accounts or Bergdorf's bill. Leave the money bragging to Donnie. First of all, in doing so you might attract someone only interested in money, but also, it's just not humble or ladylike to brag.

4. **Their finances.** By all means, do NOT question your date about his finances. He may think you're trying to get his money and that you're a diva in dire need.

5. **How your kids are perfect.** Just don't. It's definitely okay to be proud, and it's even okay to pull out a few photos, but nobody is perfect. If you dwell on your son too much, it may kill the mood and even create a feeling of competition if your date also has children. No matter how much you want to go on and on, bite your lip.

6. **Your health.** Normally, this would only come up if you're in bad health or have health issues. Please keep in mind that health struggles are better discussed with your doctor or your close friends. Spare your first date the horror of your colonoscopy or your hemorrhoidectomy.

Melly dear, if the thought of a new relationship scares the bejeebies out of you (and gives you butterflies), hold my advice in all of these letters close to your heart and let me say, "Good luck" to you. You deserve it!

In love and friendship forever,

Ms. Priscilla Purity

www.ingramcontent.com/pod-product-compliance
Lightning Source LLC
Chambersburg PA
CBHW071302130626
46556CB00003B/1437